In the Valley of the Ancients

A Book of Native American Legends

by Lou Cuevas

Illustrated by Jim Fuge

Southwest Parks and
Monuments Association

Tucson, Arizona

Library of Congress Cataloging-in-Publication Data
Cuevas, Lou, 1946
  In the valley of the ancients: a book of Native
  American legends
  Lou Cuevas: illustrated by Jim Fuge.
    p. cm.
  Originally published: Albuquerque, N.M.: Petroglyph
  National Monument, [1996].
  ISBN 1-877856-82-7
  Indians of North America—Southwest, New—
  Folklore. 2. Indian mythology—Southwest, New.
  3. Tales—Southwest, New. I. Title.
  E78.S7C76 1997
  398.2"097—dc21   97–3439
                        CIP

Copyright © 1997 by Lou Cuevas
Published by Southwest Parks and Monuments Association
The net proceeds from SPMA publications support educa-
tional and research programs in the national parks.

Receive a free Southwest Parks and Monuments Association
catalog, featuring hundreds of publications.
Email: info@spma.org

Edited by Robin White
Cover design by Mo Martin
Text designed by Sandra Hilton
Printing by Arizona Lithographers
♲ Printed on recycled paper with
inks from renewable resources

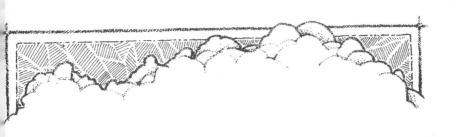

With thanks to Park Ranger Robin White,
who contributed her time and talent
to make this book possible.

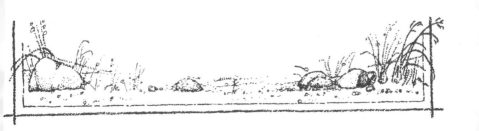

Table of Contents

Introduction

Legends take us back to the origins of the tribal people, to their hopes, struggles and defeats. There are many cultures which have stories that are not readily available in print. The information is not found in libraries, but exists within the hearts and minds of individuals called Storytellers.

Legends are a celebration of the human spirit, part of our American tradition, and the history of our country. To this very day they are being told, altered, and retold. In this book, the author attempts to present an interesting version of chanted literature. The legends are told in his voice, echoing the voices of his ancestors. The author does not attempt to present the only account or version of the legends, nor does he wish to offend similar tribal Storytellers. If the reader enjoys these myths, the author in retelling them has achieved his purpose.

It is important to understand the roles and power of the Storyteller. These oral historians are given the responsibility of remembering and reciting their Native American Culture. It is through their ability that we understand their true heritage.

The Yellow Flower

The land of the Ancient Ones once covered the United States. They were the first humans to walk across North and South America. Despite the distance, many tribes had much in common: their clothing, hair styles, food, religion and beliefs. But their strongest bond was their history. Among Indian legends are found many stories which connect tribal origins.

You will now learn of Yellow Flower. Travel to the Northwest, where she was called Rain Woman. Journey to the Midwest where she earned the name of Corn Woman. Visit the Southwest, and Changing Woman will come, and in Central America, she was known as Jaguar Woman. This mythical being suffered many hardships in order to bring happiness to others.

The practice of slavery existed among the American Indians long before the Europeans refined it. It was not uncommon for members of a tribe - either through war, poverty or trade - to lose ownership of their lives.

Once there was a slave called Chi'ane, which means flower in the sun. She was born the daughter of a Chieftain, and by birth was a Princess. At the age of fifteen her people lost an important war, which caused a dreadful change in her life.

Chi'ane was sold into bondage, and taken to the North Country, where she became the property of the Black Stone People. Day after day, she worked hard only to receive scraps of food. The desert days were hot and the nights cold. One night as she wept, a spirit visited her and promised that one day she would bring joy to people everywhere.

Days later a great drought descended upon the land. The

skies refused to cool the scorching desert as people, crops, and animals died. Because Chi'ane was a stranger in the village she was accused of causing such doom. The Medicine Man, foreseeing the reaction of his people, took Chi'ane to the crop fields and begged her to pray. Fearing death, she desperately prayed to the Great Spirit for rain.

As Chi'ane prayed, her crystal-like tears fell gently upon the earth, and it began to rain. The people were so happy they gave thanks to the Great Spirit and adopted her. Chi'ane's remaining years were blessed with a rewarding life. When she died a tall yellow flower grew where she was buried. The Black Stone People gave the flower seeds to their children. The seeds bloomed into a beautiful flower that springs forth annually. Today it is known as the *Sun Flower*.

One of the many elements within the
cycle of life is soil, a fertile bed which
brings forth new life. But it too,
must be nurtured.

The White Shield

Across the pages of Indian lore are written the ancient sagas of the Native American. The stories are delivered in the voice of the Storyteller, who is a caretaker of the tribe's heritage. To become a Storyteller one must be chosen by, and learn from, an elder of the tribe. Such was the tale of Little Wolf of the Black Shell People.

One day Little Wolf's father and others went on a hunting trip and became lost. When his father and others did not return, a second group was sent in search of them. But, they too failed to return.

During this crisis Little Wolf went to live with his grandparents. His Grandmother taught him how to care for himself against numerous ills, and his Grandfather taught him stories of the tribe's history. As the weeks passed, Little Wolf learned of his ancestors, their courage, unbending spirit, achievements and losses. Little Wolf soon possessed the oral history of his people within him; his greatest responsibility was to remember it always.

As his people had not received word from the second hunting party, a third group was assembled, and Little Wolf volunteered to go. He and twenty men went forward to learn what had happened to their loved ones.

They traveled for two weeks, and were on the open range when they discovered the weather was changing. Cold winds replaced the warm air. The bright sunlight dimmed and it began to snow. Half the group returned to the camp for additional supplies, as they were not adequately prepared for the cold weather.

As sundown neared, Little Wolf discovered he was lost. The snow fell harder and harder as he struggled forward with great difficulty, until he was unable to go any further. Suddenly he encountered a beautiful maiden. Little Wolf knew instantly that she was a Spirit. He recalled his Grandfather's words that spiritual beings can cause changes in the weather. The young maiden wore clothing suited for summer, yet she did not appear to be affected by the falling snow.

Shivering, Little Wolf neared the maiden and asked, "How can I help you?"

"I'm looking for my mother's shield," she laughed playfully.

"What does it look like?" asked Little Wolf seriously.

"It is oval shaped, white, and designed to protect me from my brother's anger," she replied.

"I will help you look for it," offered Little Wolf, "if you will tell me where I can find my people.

"Agreed!" the spirit answered as if playing a game. As the maiden danced atop the snow, she asked Little Wolf about his people.

Little Wolf proudly began to tell the story of his people with much enthusiasm. As the maiden listened, his stories created vivid images in her mind. Some of the tales caused the maiden to cry. With others she was inspired or captured in deep thought, and many filled her with joy. When he finished his stories, the maid quickly reached into the snow covered ground, pulled up a flower and gave it to Little Wolf. "You have earned a special gift for the memory of your people which lives within your heart," she said.

Little Wolf was overwhelmed. As he put the flower in his pouch, a beam of sunlight appeared near the spirit. The maiden immediately fell to the earth in agony and began to scream. Little Wolf felt the warmth of the sun and could not understand why she was in such pain. Quickly he knelt and anxiously began throwing handfuls of snow on the screaming maiden. Suddenly, there was silence. As the dark passing clouds again blocked the sunlight, the maiden arose from beneath the shield and thanked Little Wolf. The spirit spoke to Little Wolf saying, "You found my mother's shield. Very few are aware that I am a daughter of the Earth Mother. It was I who took away the spring weather and threw my mother's white shield across the earth. Now my brother the sun reminds me to return to my sleep. I thank you for your kindness, but I must go now."

"What about my father and my people?" reminded Little Wolf.

"They were trapped by the blizzard when I came up to play," said the Spirit.

"They shall be released and blessed with a successful hunt. I have learned how important they and your people are from your stories."

The Spirit, and with her the winter season, soon disappeared. Little Wolf and his friends returned home. The first two hunting parties arrived at the camp with enough food to celebrate with a feast. From that day forward, the importance of the storyteller was evident. As for the flower given as a gift to Little Wolf, the Indians called it *The Snow Flower* (Cereus). It blooms only during the cold of winter.

The Four Spears

The wise ones say the ancient ways are written in the sky. It is believed by many indigenous People that one need only look to the earth, the water and sky spirits, to see their heritage. To better understand the people that inhabited the land before time, one must hear the Legend of the Four Spears.

Long ago, in a place called the Dwelling, there lived a people who were known as the Pintos, or Painted Ones. They practiced the art of painting their bodies. Each individual of the tribe had a particular color or design which identified him or his family.

Within the tribe were a proud couple who raised four extraordinary sons. The oldest was called Red Bird, next was Yellow Horse, followed by Blue Hand and the youngest was known as Green Knife. They were tall, strong and famed for their courage. The four were inseparable.

The unity between the four brothers served them well against envy from others. It was their father, upon seeing his sons fighting their enemies, who predicted that their combined strength would one day bring everlasting honor. To confirm their father's prediction the boys decided to visit the wisest man in the tribe - the Shaman.

With a gift in hand, the Four Brothers sat outside the tepee of the Shaman, until they were invited into the Medicine Lodge. The Shaman accepted their generous offering, as was the custom. He then asked, "What is it that you boys desire to know?" Red Wolf asked if he and his brothers would always be together. The Shaman requested the brothers draw some soot from the smoldering fire. Thereafter the Shaman read the ashen imprint in their hands and told them that their future would be written in the sky.

Not long after the visit, trouble arrived in the Dwelling. A neighboring tribe brought war to their villages. The four brothers joined their tribal brothers in combat. They were confident, and were seen recklessly endangering their lives in every confrontation. Their strength and courage became the main reason the enemy could not defeat the Pintos. It came to the enemy leader that he must destroy the four brothers to capture the village.

Some unprepared Pintos were lured into an ambush and taken prisoner. Upon learning of their peoples capture, the four brothers walked unafraid into the enemy camp and requested the freedom of the captives. They openly challenged the enemy to a contest. Of course, the enemy accepted. The Chief of the enemy tribe chose four of his bravest men, and the brothers were taken to a monstrous waterfall.

Chanting his death song, Red Bird wished his brothers well and promised to meet them in the spirit world. He hurled his spear into the misted sky and dove into the waterfall where he immediately disappeared. The enemy warriors, seeing the horrible death of the challenger, begged their Chief to be spared such an awful death.

The enemy Chief, ashamed of their cowardice, asked the forgiveness of the remaining brothers and set them free. The brothers forgave the enemy Chief, gave out a war cry, hurled their colorful spears into the sky, and followed their brother into the roaring waterfall.

Magically, it began to rain as the last brother disappeared.

The entire village was covered with a fine mist as the enemy Chief hung his head, wondering if such bravery would ever be remembered.

The Shaman of the Pintos, who had accompanied the four brothers, came forward to address the Chief. He informed the enemy Chief that the four brothers were predestined to always be together. "Their lives were bound by honor and courage," he said. The Chief asked, "Has not death separated them?" The Shaman pointed up into the misty sky, and everyone observed that the brothers had left their bright spear marks streaking across the sky to form the first rainbow.

Unity among the tribal people was a concept understood and accepted by all. The idea that there is strength in unity was a common belief. A good example of this is trying to break a single twig when it is in the company of ten.

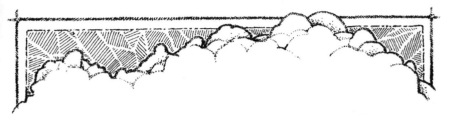

Legend of the Magic Riddle

Since the beginning, mankind has been plagued by an inescapable enemy, which is time. It is not so much its measurement, but rather its uncertainty. Man has always been consumed by the mystery of who did what first.

In the sagas of Native American Mythology, there exists a legend of how a clan living in what was then called the .ja-se-jo, or the House of the Red Snake, met the challenge of the time. There are many people who take part in this story, yet the most central figures are a man named Dancing Bear, and a woman called Little Dove. The story originates twenty years prior to their birth. Their parents and tribe members were living near the Little Snake River...

The harsh winter months had begun to loosen their grip allowing the valley people to take great joy in their hunting and gathering expeditions. On one particular day amid those returning from such an expedition, it was noted that a stranger walked among them. Many were startled by his sudden appearance and lack of fatigue. The hunters gathered slowly unto themselves to discuss the stranger. His clothes appeared new; and though his dress was similar, they could not identify him. The stranger was allowed to enter their camp because it was their custom to take no action against strangers without first consulting with the Chief.

The elders eyed him with suspicion and caution, the younger men were curious. Children were gathered by the women as the village began to buzz about the arrival of the stranger. The Chief, council members and Shaman were disturbed by the stranger, but hid their emotions behind stern masks of patience.

Unhindered, the stranger walked slowly toward the council grounds. The Chief noted that the stranger appeared to be an old man, but reflected a youthful aura. The visitor appeared indifferent to the people surrounding him as he sat down near the council fire. The Chief sat directly across from him, and the braves of the tribe formed a half circle behind their Chief.

The visitor spoke softly asking, "Are you the leader of these people?"

"I am called Little Crow," answered the Chief. He was surprised that the visitor could speak their language so flawlessly.

"Then, Little Crow, I have a question for you and your people," the visitor said. "Do you wish to live in peace on this land?"

"Can it be otherwise?" the Chief replied curiously. "Can you alter the fate of our children or their future?"

"One easily becomes the other," answered the visitor. "I have come to your people with a riddle. Fail to answer it and you will die unknown. Solve it, and your people will live as one with Mother Earth."

"What is this riddle?" asked Little Crow.

"Before any attempt is made to answer," the visitor replied glancing at the entire circle of people, "you must first choose two from among your people to bear the responsibility of failure. With each attempt, I will require a price. Since you are the leaders of your people, you must choose one man and one woman. The others will face their fate in time. Do you accept these conditions?"

"They are harsh," complained the Chief. "If we are to take you seriously," he continued, "give us some proof that we are not being made sport of."

"One of your older women has in her care a sightless child named Dark Cloud. Is this not true?" asked the visitor.

The woman stepped forward from the crowd and replied, "My child has been blind since birth, five winters now."

"Take the child to the river," ordered the visitor. "Reach into the stream and touch his eyes with the waters."

The woman all but drowned herself and the child as they fell kneeling at the river's edge. With her heart pounding, she reached into the cool waters with a cupped hand and bathed her son's eyes. The child began to cry, then, with sight restored, ran among the people, who watched with amazement. Many were now convinced that the visitor was more than he seemed, perhaps a powerful spirit.

"When must you have our decision?" questioned the Chief.

"I shall sit here and wait for your answer," replied the visitor. "I am prepared to wait until you are ready."

After a brief discussion, the council favored accepting the challenge. The Chief agreed, and prayed the answer was within their collective wisdom. Returning to the visitor with a young man and woman, the Chief advised the visitor that they would accept his terms, and the riddle.

The visitor stood and directed his words to the surrounding crowd. "I give you this riddle that you may win a place in the future. It will determine what you will inherit. I offer one clue in the hope it may aid you. Your mother gave you life, your father nurtured it, and all children will return to their parents. Here is the riddle. From the water rises the land, the symbol of your father; the spirit of their song is the shield of your mother."

"Is this your riddle?" questioned the astonished Chief.

"It is," stated the visitor without emotion.

"How much time do we have to respond with the answer?" asked the Chief with deep concern.

"One day," was the visitor's reply.

The people were baffled by the riddle. The following day the best answer the tribe could give was "a mountain." It was not the answer, and the first two lives belonged to the visitor.

"I will return in the cycle of one moon," he said. "You have until then to solve the riddle."

It was advised to draw names from the pottery jar from which the next pair would be chosen.

Month after month, always on the new cycle, the visitor returned to hear a measure of different answers. "It's a beaver!" tried one. "It's a tree!" attempted another. Not one of the answers were correct. No one dared to inquire about the victims, whom many believed were killed and eaten. Year after year they dwindled, becoming a smaller and smaller community. Each cycle of the moon produced fear, and the appearance of the visitor doubled their anxiety. Still no one could be found who could solve the riddle.

Twenty years passed, and life in the camp settled miserably around a single cyclical event. It was taken for granted that two people would be lost each month. The years had not altered the visitor in any way. He had not aged, nor had his power diminished.

Throughout the two decades many children were born. Among the newborn were two bright, intuitive youngsters who seemed to possess no fear of the visitor, despite the worries and troubles of their parents. They were named according to their dispositions - the boy they named Dancing Bear, the girl was called Little Dove. As the children blossomed they were made aware of the riddle and the risk everyone faced. Still, they remained unafraid. Indeed, as they matured, they too placed their name in the pottery jar from which all the pairs were chosen. Like all those before them, they swore to abide by the choice of the council and their Chief.

Dancing Bear and Little Dove took the complex riddle seriously. Yet, they too became accustomed to seeing the visitor return, recite his riddle and then depart with two of their friends. Unable to help, they vowed to someday learn the answer. Planting season arrived, as well as migrating tribes. The people hoped the newcomers would become their allies and help solve the riddle. But the newcomers repeatedly attacked and burned the village, conquering the Chief, council members and others who remained. It was then that the courage and wisdom of Dancing Bear surfaced as their new leader.

Dancing Bear relocated his people, seeking protection in the cliffs. During the following weeks Dancing Bear believed he had stored sufficient supplies to redress his enemy. He departed, bidding farewell to his people. Dancing Bear and his men soon reached the lower woods. Surrounded by an enemy who blocked his escape, Dancing Bear and his group took defensive positions along the wide river, seeking refuge among the enormous boulders that night. A short distance away, Little Dove slipped into his camp. Dancing Bear suggested that Little Dove leave quickly to escape, but she refused.

The following day, as Dancing Bear sat idly by the river, a huge turtle swam by. It crawled upon the embankment as it ventured out of the water. Little Dove recognized it as a source of food, cooked it, and fashioned the shell into a shield. An hour after the band had eaten the great turtle, their spirits began to rise. Feeling a new source of strength, Dancing Bear instructed his men to chant. The chant and songs attracted the attention of the surrounding invaders.

The enemy Chief challenged Dancing Bear to single combat. Dancing Bear selected the turtle shell as a shield, and he defeated the enemy Chief in battle in the shallow water. Seeing their great Chief slain in battle, the remaining invaders fled into the woods. Not long after the defeat of the invaders, Dancing Bear and his people returned to their land and rebuilt their village.

The visitor entered the rebuilt camp, and as before sat down near the council fire. "Tell me young Chief," began the stranger with noticeable price, "what is the answer to this riddle? From the water rises the land, the symbol of your fathers; the spirit of their song is the shield of your mother."

"The answer, old one, is a turtle," began Dancing Bear with confidence. "It rose from the water onto the land. It has always been a powerful symbol of our fathers. The turtle's spirit gave me courage, and I expressed it in a song. In the turtle's armor, I saw the shield of my mother the earth." The entire tribe had gathered to hear the answer offered to the visitor. It was an answer which only Dancing Bear and Little Dove had determined, as they conversed at length about the events near the river.

The stranger allowed everyone to hold their breath a bit longer before he smiled and acknowledged that Dancing Bear had given the correct answer. Though Dancing Bear was glad, he sadly remarked that "we cannot still time, nor does time wait on anyone." The answer so long in arriving had cost the lives of too many of his people.

"They never died, young man," explained the visitor. "I only took them to other parts of this land to become the parents of new tribes. You and Little Dove shall enjoy the answer to this riddle as a gift for all time. Your people shall have many children in generations to come."

Dancing Bear surmised that the visitor had given the tribe the answer when he first arrived. "The Earth Spirit gives life to all inhabitants, and it is the Sky Father who nurtures it," he explained. Dancing Bear was not one to forget such a memorable fight as the one he had had with the enemy Chief. He had encountered death, and knew upon waking that all life will eventually return to their parents, the Earth and Sky.

The Sacred Stone

Tribes of the Rio Grande Valley, like their ancestors, have always believed no one owned the land - it belonged to everyone. They knew the four corners of the earth arose from here. Their religious mythology centered on numbers, colors and stages of life. To them the desert valley, which is called the Rio Grande, was the very essence of all they held sacred. Take for instance the story of a woman who was created to record the history of the desert tribes. Her legend is one of many in the Southwest.

The woman's name was Boca, which means sacred voice, or one who speaks through her mouth. She was born to the desert. Her tribe, called the Wanderers, lived in the Rio Grande Valley two thousand years ago.

The Wanderers were not looking for a permanent home. Their mission in life was to befriend their neighbors and teach others the skills of hunting, fishing, trapping, pottery making, basket weaving and farming. No warriors existed in the Wanderer's tribe.

The Wanderers sent ambassadors to let other tribes know of their peaceful intentions. If the neighboring tribes were receptive, the ambassadors would stay with them and teach them about spirituality. Some aggressor clans wanted to study the arts of war, which was a skill the Wanderers did not possess. Yet many desert tribes were pleased with the Wanderers peaceful nature, and often adopted the peaceful practices of their teachers.

This was how Boca came to live with the valley people. She was quite content to stay and teach them, but in time she realized that the people of the valley were not interested in what she offered. They spent more time raiding and stealing than farming and hunting. Boca expressed sorrow that the people were creating a lasting hatred among the other tribes, and tried to discourage war.

After several years of war the valley people were surprised by their declined population. In desperation, they asked Boca if she would go to their enemy camp and ask for peace. This Boca did with joy.

When the tribes sent their ambassadors, those whom they talked to often demonstrated a lack of trust to ensure their own safety. The Hill tribe, the Mountain tribe, the River tribe, the Valley tribe, and the smaller clans were so scattered that it took weeks for Boca to get them to council. When everyone finally came together, Boca spent a great deal of time and patience trying to please each tribe. As she secured one condition, another tribe refused it. When she succeeded in changing it, the other tribe protested. Still she journeyed from tribe to tribe doing her best. Finally, the tribes were convinced by her to demonstrate their desire to live in peace. They were to meet and sign their symbol of peace in stone.

But when the tribes met on that great day of hope, they fell in and began to quarrel. In the center of the fiercest fighting was Boca. The Great Spirit saw that she was in danger of being killed, and sealed her inside a great round stone for protection. Weeks later when the tribes had stopped their bloody conflict, hundreds of lives were found to have been lost.

Legend has it that the Great Spirit wanted Boca to continue her peaceful work and to continue to visit every nation on the planet. The great stone upon which peace will eventually be signed is still carried by her. As a matter of fact, it became her home. Today she is considered to be the sign of good fortune. Among some petroglyphs you will see animals enclosed in protective shields. It is told that the shields are their homes.

Nearly all Native American tribes believed in living in peace. Most of their legends center on this one element. It was sacrilegious to break a promise or a treaty.

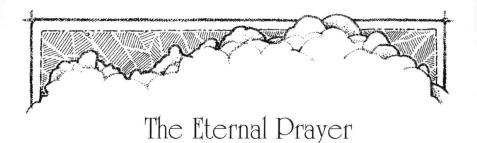

The Eternal Prayer

The Rio Grande River is the reason there are villages, pueblos and life in the desert. In the city of Albuquerque there is a legend as to why this place came to be. Several tribes recall the story, but none are alike. One story is remembered as the Eternal Prayer . . .

Long before the Europeans reached the Southwest, tribes of an ancient people existed. They traveled the desert, perhaps looking for a permanent home. They were a proud and arrogant group, and gave little acknowledgment to Father Sky. He was the Creator and tried to impress upon their hearts and minds the goodness which could help them become spiritually oriented people. They were aware of the Sky Father's many gifts, but failed to thank him for their blessings. In addition, they felt he owed them, and that it was his duty to provide everything they wished for. With great patience Sky Father continued to provide his children gifts from the earth.

The people made their homes near the river. Father Sky taught them to live in harmony with the earth and each other. He only requested that they give thanks for their gifts, and never take any animal or human life for granted -- because, whatever people take from nature, must also come with responsibility. Humans must always respect Mother Earth and her inhabitants.

It was unfortunate for the tribe that they did not bear in mind Sky Father's wishes. Mother Earth was at their disposal, to do with as they wished. Perhaps they felt superior to all other life, and that is why the people did not wish to give thanks for their daily blessings. They continued to live in the river valley with a fragrance of conceit. They refused to give thanks or accept the responsibility to provide a little care for Mother Earth.

This selfish behavior saddened Sky Father. One day as the people gathered along the river's edge, Sky Father appeared and reminded them of all they had received. Yet even as he spoke to the people, he witnessed the indifference of his children. They were unyielding, taking the gift of life itself, their neighbors, family members, Mother Earth and all her inhabitants for granted. Sky Father pledged that if they would not give thanks for a few minutes a day, then they would do so forever. So saying, he transformed all of the river people into trees with their hands extending up into the sky.

Today, many tribes believe the trees are a reminder that mankind has an important role in nature. They remind us if we take from nature, we must give something back. If we do not give thanks now, we may never be able to do so. The people in the story refused to give thanks. Now they have eternity to do so.

Among some tribes there is a saying: "Life is brief, but long is the sleep in the ground. Treat your bed with respect, so that your rest may come without regret."

Legend of the Snow Giants

Long before mankind began, there existed a time with no recorded dates. The ancient N'De, (an Apache term meaning the People) spoke of the Age of the Snow World. The ancient ones tell of a great race of giants who ruled the early primal earth. Legend places these giants here long before the first humans were created.

According to the ancients, when the Sky Father created the planet earth, he also created a powerful race of beings that were suppose to live amongst one another in harmony. They were known as the Earth Children. In the passage of time, Sky Father bestowed on them wondrous gifts.

Among the powers given them was the gift of immortality. Their lives would last a million years. Their gigantic bodies were made of ice and snow, with thick outer layers of blue sheeting. Their massive forms, which often reached some ten thousand feet high, were able to withstand considerable impact. Although made of ice and snow, the giants were said to have lungs capable of breathing and producing liquid fire. They ate enormous quantities of earth from which they took their nourishment.

In the beginning the giants were content. But as the ages passed, some of the giants grew to believe themselves superior and invincible to everything around them. They suspiciously believed that the Sky Father had given them only a few of the precious gifts of life. They grumbled that he had kept the best for himself. Thus convinced, they conspired against their father, however, some of the giants remained grateful to their creator for his generosity. When they learned that their brothers had grown contemptuous and were plotting to challenge their father, they gave over to defend him. Thus the war of the Snow Giants began.

The earth, as the giants knew it, was a flat surface. They could travel in any direction for months at a time and never sight any landmarks. For them, the planet was simply a place to eat and sleep. From horizon to horizon there was but one boundary hemming the land together; this was the waters of Keeka. She was the spirit sister of all water forces, and would one day become the mother of mankind. The snow giants feared Keeka, because if she ever touched them she could seize their immortality. Even though they could never die, she could feed on them for centuries and cause erosion. Because of her power, they stayed within their boundaries.

For the Snow Giants there was only one place to live and that was on the single continent called the Great Circle. This then was the battlefield upon which the war of the Snow Giants would be fought. Once the family of Earth Children divided according to loyalty, the battle was begun. When the giants began their war there was no one to prevent them from continuing it. However in the giant's battles, they discovered something very interesting. When angered, any one of these towering ice giants could explode in a raging fit of temper causing him to exhale a million tons of fiery liquid onto an opponent. The effects were destructive. Although the land was empty, it soon came to be marred with hundreds and thousands of huge slag heaps. These enormous mounds were the remains of the fallen Snow Giants.

The Sky Father asked the two sides to stop. One side obeyed, however the other side would not, giving the defenders reason to renew their war. Finally, Sky Father used his great powers to separate the Earth Children. While the two sides slept, he divided the earth's continents into several large pieces. This allowed Keeka to move in between the continents. Now in order to fight one another the giants would have to enter her domain, and they were well aware of what would happen if they did.

When the rebellious giants awoke, they were ready to continue the battle. With weapons in hand they searched for their opponents. However they soon realized that none could be found. Their anger increased as their vain search dragged on for months. When the rebellious giants located their adversaries, they were astonished. They were positioned across the wide gulf of Keeka. From both shores the giants eyed each other, but none could bridge the distance.

In the following decades these continents remained quiet. But instead of enjoying peace the giants sat about disgruntled, thinking how to reach the other side of the world. In time, they decided to try the impossible to reach their enemy. While the more peaceful Snow Giants discussed the forthcoming attack, the quarrelsome ones across the gulf chose some of their bravest people to challenge Keeka and defeat her. Surely with so many attempting to destroy her, one of their members would succeed.

Keeka caused the first assault group of Giants in the southern portion of the planet to freeze instantly, creating the continent of Antarctica. Those who attacked from the north were frozen to form the northern polar regions. The remaining Giants who attacked from the center continents sank immediately to become the ocean's underwater mountains. With almost no effort, Keeka remained unconquered.

Sky Father turned to the Snow Giants that defended him. To this day, their presence can be seen as the world's highest peaks. Mankind knows them as the Atlas Mountains in Africa, the Himalayas and the Swiss Alps. Still many others were transformed into the Rockies of North America. Wherever the Sky Father put them, he allowed a heavy mantle of ice and snow to rest on their massive shoulders allowing the world to witness a Snow Giant.

Though the Sky Father was saddened by this grave task, he was determined to end the senseless fighting. When at last he had changed the last of the loyal ones into mountains, he returned to his sky home. There he created a race of children to whom he would entrust the whole planet. He made them tiny and very fragile. He called them N'De, the People.

Remaining rebellious Giants came out of hiding and called Sky Father to battle. Sky Father met the Snow Giants in hand to hand combat in the black stormy skies above the earth. The enraged Snow Giant's icy bodies were smashed into trillions of tiny fragments. When the fight was over Sky Father allowed the winds to sweep the fragments away.

Down on the planet's surface, the people were awed by the falling debris. The earthly inhabitants were witnessing the giant's final battle. In passing years, they marked this event as winter and the falling remains of the Snow Giants were called snow tears. Today we call them snowflakes.

Legend of the Golden Eagle

These people were the forbearers of the Apache nation. From them came the knowledge of every creature's origin.

The N'De had a special relationship with the Giver of Life. As they kept his laws, he blessed them with gifts. At various times throughout the year, the N'De would gather to celebrate and give thanks.

Long ago, there had been good years and the N'De had prospered well in the land of their fathers. For twelve turns of the snow, they enjoyed their blessings. As the N'De prepared to celebrate the time of trail (the change from boyhood to manhood), far off to the north a powerful tribe was bringing their war to the south.

Among the boys who hoped to take their place in the ranks of the N'De warriors was a lad named Cloud Dancer. During the third week of his travel into the high mountains while wading a shallow river, Cloud Dancer froze in his tracks. His father, seeing this, looked at the reflection below his son and was astonished to see a glowing, golden image. In the river's reflection they saw a golden bird flying across a body of water, carrying a woman in its great talons.

Upon their return to the village, the boy went directly to the Medicine Man's lodge. Before the brightly painted tepee the boy placed a large cut of fresh deer meat, took up a sitting position a dozen feet from the entrance, and waited.

The boy spent most of the morning and part of the after-
noon in silence. Shortly before sunset Grandmother invited
him in and accepted the offering. She led the boy to a place
near a small fire in the center of the lodge and indicated for
him to sit directly in front of the Medicine Man.

The old man asked, "Why are you afraid of your spirit my
son?"

Cloud Dancer replied, "I only wish to understand what it
means, Grandfather."

"The images concern your destiny," explained Grandfather,
"You must be patient. Do not fear it, nor yourself. Father Sky
sends these words to you: Out of darkness will come the fire.
Flames will bring suffering, pain and anguish. Courage is the
shield of the warrior. You are the shield of your people. Ap-
proach the new moon and be born in the waters of conflict."

Cloud Dancer knew from this that he was destined to care
for his people.

During the final time of trail ceremony several tribesmen
voiced their concern to the Chief about Cloud Dancer. They
feared the water vision presented an evil spirit who would
doom the people of the village. Grandfather spoke in a soft
rumbling voice, "The vision of the golden bird was first shown
to me many moons ago. He is one of us and will bring fear to
our enemies. Cloud Dancer will stay," announced the Chief.
Although the tribe was quite troubled by what the Chief decided, the law of their tribe forbade them to dishonor him with
further protest.

Life became a series of hardships for Cloud Dancer and his
family. They were planning to go into the hills the night the

enemy from the north arrived on the outskirts of their village. The enemy took the N'De camp by surprise. Everywhere was the cry of war as the N'De tried to protect their village. With his painted war club in hand Cloud Dancer joined his brothers in battle and proved to be a great warrior. Grandfather informed Cloud Dancer that he was a different type of warrior, and must now use his gift.

While the enemy retreated to prepare for another attack the Chief ordered the tribe to cross the river in their canoes. They discovered that the river had risen, and it swept their canoes downstream. As the N'De warriors waited for the next attack on their village, the women at the river began chanting their prayers to Sky Father. The tribe was sure that death was just moments away.

Cloud Dancer was standing at the river when he began to transform into a golden image. There in the pitch black night, the Chief saw a magnificent golden bird with huge ivory talons flying above him. In his talons, he saw groups of screaming women and children being taken across the wide river to safety. Upon setting one group down, the great bird flew back across for another group. The enemy, who by now had broken through, arrived to behold the golden bird. So terrified were they of the screaming golden creature that many were trampled by their own numbers. Many more were injured by the great wind caused by the bird's wings.

The remaining enemies were driven out of the camp, with the N'De chasing them and the golden bird flying above them. There was much joy in the N'De victory and sadness when the fiery bird flew off into the night.

It took the N'De people many months to regain their life of

peace. Yet when the year had come full circle, the summer hunt was given a new meaning. A special dance in memory of their fallen warriors was introduced, and a celebration of the creation of the Golden Eagle was held.

Many years have passed, yet to this day, the Apache Indians still celebrate the Golden Eagle in ceremonial chants and songs. The dance is still one most often performed at the beginning of the summer festivals.

Shi-A-Lee

The ancient N'De claimed the open territories of the Southwest as their birthright. Despite their many travels, their way of life changed little from generation to generation. The legend of Shi-a-lee was said to originate with a small band of N'De who, for several seasons, lived near what today is known as the Big Snake Mountain.

Shi-a-lee traveled to the river to draw water. On her way she passed her best friend, Kema, who joined her at the river. They discussed who Shi-a-lee's father might marry her to. Shi-a-lee assured Kema that her father was wise and would do what was best for her. "I wish my father was that wise," sighed Kema, leaving Shi-a-lee at the edge of the river.

Shi-a-lee lifted the two jars of water preparing to return home. Suddenly, she dropped both jars to the ground as she encountered a vision of smoke filled light. Daylight was bathing the surrounding forest, and yet Shi-a-lee was determined to look directly into the cloud of smoke. It was huge, and lay across her path like an uncoiling snake. Deep from within the cloud's center a figure began to appear. It was a man. Shi-a-lee's eyes widened, and feeling dizzy, she fainted.

Several minutes later she felt the coolness of water droplets touch her face. It was being sprinkled from her best friend's hand. "Are you alright?" asked Kema. "When I saw you had not returned from the river, I came back to see what was keeping you." Shi-a-lee said nothing, thinking that people might say she was crazy.

That night Shi-a-lee took her mother aside and related her story in great detail. There is but one man who can explain, advised the mother. Shi-a-lee took a ram skin coat and placed it outside the Medicine Man's lodge. Her wait was not long and soon she sat before the Medicine Man relating her vision. "From the inside of a cloud, a bright light came forth and turned into a man. He was an old man, someone whom I have never seen, yet, I thought for a moment that I knew him."

"Did he say anything?" questioned the old one.

"He said I was his woman, that I have always belonged to him."

"Listen closely, my child," related the wise one, "You had a vision. I assure you, it will return again and again."

It was not long after her encounter at the river's edge that Shi-a-lee was asked to come to her father's tepee. Upon arriving, she saw standing near her father the son of Dark Moon, the warrior. Many times she had seen him, and like other girls her age, had come to whisper his name. "I am called Little Wolf," stated the lad. "I am the eldest son of Dark Moon, my father, and White Bird, my mother. I come to you, and ask that my gifts be accepted for the hand of your daughter Shi-a-lee. It is my desire that she be my wife."

"What do you offer besides your many gifts that will promise happiness for my daughter?" questioned Two Bears.

"I am a hunter, and warrior of our people," defended Little Wolf. "I will try to be what you would ask of a son. I will bring no disgrace upon you."

The wedding day of Shi-a-lee was fixed. With the appearance of the new moon, she would be married. During that time, Little Wolf was permitted to court his intended. As time passed, Shi-a-lee allowed herself to be won by the romantically driven Little Wolf. Yet, in her heart there lingered the memory of the visitor by the river. When at last the vision did return, Shi-a-lee was prepared. This time the image was more vivid. The young maid was determined to gain more details. "You have always been mine!" said the vision.

Not long after, Shi-a-lee was married and, true to his word, Little Wolf proved to be an honorable husband. In terms of custom, tradition and necessary essentials, the newlyweds were very fortunate. The happiness which Shi-a-lee and Little Wolf experienced multiplied dramatically with the birth of their first son. However, with him also came responsibilities and additional worries as they joined the rest of the tribe in preparing for the changing days. Season followed season, and with each change of the year their abilities to care for each other and their growing family were tested and retested.

One day, while walking, the vision returned. There standing before her within the cloud of smoke, a figure of an aged N'De warrior stepped forth. This time, as the vision spoke to her, Shi-a-lee studied the face intently. She saw that the man's eyes were familiar. Despite the fact that the figure was near seventy, his face seemed to belong to someone whom she should recognize. She concentrated hard, but the image disappeared. Shi-a-lee was sure he was no longer a threat, and a feeling of confidence swept over her. Nearly fifty years had passed since Shi-a-lee had become the bride of Little Wolf. Having raised five children, and buried three, she was aware of the shortness of life. She had experienced the pain of her parent's death, and witnessed many relatives and friends depart under the many wars which effected the peaceful tribe. Shi-a-lee was a different woman - dignified, like a great oak tree. Her heart still beat with love for her husband, but she had seen him harden with every new conflict. She had also seen her tribe's land shrink with the influx of new people. There was much sorrow in her memory.

In her sixty-fifth year, in the middle of what would later be known as winter's last snow storm, Shi-a-lee took ill. The storm was severe, and four long days Shi-a-lee suffered. On the fifth day the storm lessened, allowing warm weather to blanket the land. When the storm passed, so too did Shi-a-lee's sickness. The days which followed were warm enough for her to be laid outside to embrace the fresh air and feel the gentleness of the sun. From here Shi-a-lee could study the whole camp. It was good to see her people working the camp.

Before long a young girl, fifteen years of age, asked for Shi-a-lee's permission to grind her corn nearby and to talk with her. Shi-a-lee eagerly consented.

"Have you had a good life Grandmother?" asked the girl.

"I have had a very good life," replied Shi-a-lee, propping herself up a bit.

"Has anything special ever happened to you?"

Before Shi-a-lee could answer the girl's question, a cooking fire was started near her tepee which created great spirals of smoke that began to uncoil before her. The morning sun was rising and gave the smoky clouds an air of mystery. Despite its harsh brightness, Shi-a-lee stared into the circle and saw a man appear from within it. Shi-a-lee smiled when she recognized the tall figure approaching her. He was an old, but fully experienced warrior. He was the Chief of the tribe. His name was Little Wolf, and as he approached, he saw that his ailing wife had recovered. Nearing his lifetime companion, he stated, "You will always be mine, I have always loved you."

With the sun at his back and the clouds of smoke about him, he was a vision to behold.

Unaware of his backdrop, he stepped through the coiling rings of smoke and knelt down next to his wife, Shi-a-lee. Gently stroking his wife's forehead, he smiled down at her. He was truly glad she had lived through her illness. "From the time when I first stood before your father's house, and until our spirits are joined together and our lives become the memories of our children, you and I are joined by our love. Never forget that, my wife." Having reaffirmed his love to her, Little Wolf rose and entered the tepee. Shi-a-lee said nothing as the mysterious vision she experienced as a child suddenly became clear. What she had witnessed throughout her life was nothing more than a premonition of her future.

"Did you, Grandmother?" repeated her Granddaughter, unaware of what had just transpired. "Did you ever have anything special happen to you?"

As Shi-a-lee looked into her Granddaughter's beautiful dark eyes she said, "No my child, nothing special. Every experience I've ever had was ordained by the Giver of Life."

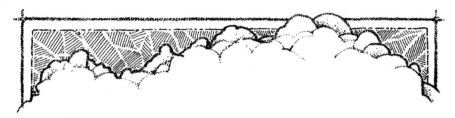

The Journey of Earth Daughter

The sandy desert of the Southwest was not known for farming, but many original crops took firm root in the very soil which makes up this open arid space. To the natives of the Southwest, planting was not an easy task. On the contrary, were it not for the two types of farming (dry and wet), there would be no farms at all. Many types of fruits and vegetables can be found in the Southwest, yet the most popular vegetable of them all is not native to the Southwest desert. Its origins arise in the dark soils of Central America. There are several versions of how this plant was brought to the Southwestern desert. Here is one version . . .

Many years ago the practice of human sacrifices was common in the Yucatan. It was a daily religious practice of the natives of Central America to offer the living hearts of victims to their sun god. Not all the tribes did so, but among the most ardent believers of this ritual were the Aztecs. They believed that the sun above their heads was powered by a mighty war god called Huitzilopochtli, who needed great amounts of power. The main source of this power came from human hearts. It is not exaggeration to say that hundreds of thousands of people were sacrificed. In order to continue this process, the Aztec nation ensured a constant war time society to provide for a steady supply of human beings for use in sacrificial ceremonies.

The surrounding tribes who lived close to the Aztecs did so in constant fear. One tribe who lived under this umbrella of terror was the Zemicos. They believed in many gods, but their most popular one was a god of the inner earth. It was she who they believed brought forth the abundance of the natural world. To her they attributed all the different types of plants which could be used for food. The children of the Zemicos were taught that if they treated the earth with prayer and kindness, the earth would yield up her riches.

Such was the belief of one little girl named Koma. It was her job to awaken with the sunrise and water the plants of her family garden. Koma grew up taking care of her family garden. Every year she, her sisters and her mother were able to harvest many baskets of food for their family. Because she and her family were subjects of the Aztec empire, they had to pay tribute, or taxes, to keep their family from being sold as slaves. Koma was nearly fifteen years of age when the rains were late. Because of the drought, water became scarce. The lack of water meant that many families would die. Times became hard for everyone, and even Koma's family could not afford to pay their tribute.

This was the greatest fear of Koma's father. When he learned his family would be sold as slaves, he took them and fled the country. They traveled north for months, and every step of the way they were followed by the pursuing Aztec guards. Finally, the father knew that he would not make it to freedom with his family. With his wife, sons and daughters, Koma's father decided to turn back and fight the Aztecs who hunted his family. However, they decided to let Koma continue her journey. Koma's family reminded her of all she had learned of the earth, and the treasure of the white corn.

Believing they had killed all of the escaping family the Aztecs turned back, allowing Koma to escape and continue her journey, which eventually led to the Rio Grande Valley. There she found a peaceful tribe who befriended her. After being adopted by them she taught the women the farming secrets she had learned as a child. This included the planting and cultivation of her corn, also called maize. In the course of years the corn not only changed in size and taste, but proved to be a crop which made many tribes wealthy. After Koma's death the people praised the Earth Spirit for sending her daughter Koma. Her secrets did not die with her. In fact, because of her, a sacred ceremony was created.

In many Southwestern tribes, the story of the young girl who escaped from the land of the war god is told to remind children of the importance of listening to their elders. This knowledge may change the lives of many. The essence of this story is that Koma brought from her country to the Southwest the one plant which has become symbolic with the power of change. Her people called it the *White Tree* - we call it Yellow Corn.

The Corn Woman story is one which has many variations. It is important to remember that the gift of corn was special not only as magical power, or as a maturing phrase in a young girl's life to adulthood, but in remembrance and respect of one's family, and wisdom of the parents.

The Four Winds

This legend tells how a desert people came to possess fire. In some clans it is called the birth of the four winds, in others it is known as the origin of wind and fire. In more traditional versions it is chanted as the creation of man. This story existed long before Christians came to change the religious beliefs of the Native Americans.

The deserts of the Southwest were not always dry. In the Before Time they were as lush and green as any private garden in the east, however, there were no humans living there. Long before man was allowed to live here the Giver of Life had to determine if they were worthy to live on the surface.

Deep inside the earth was a great ocean of darkness where many different beings lived. None of them were people as we know them today - the inhabitants who lived here were only dreams, images and sketchy outlines of living things. Some were plants, trees or various animals. Other beings were only signs, numbers, omens and spirits.

Of all the underworld figures which lived in the world of darkness, only one possessed an awareness of being alive. This being was called Dream Shadow. He was told that he would never leave the dark underworld. But because his heart was strong and good, the Giver of Life changed him from dark matter into a man, and gave him a wife called Shadow Woman. Although they could not see, they knew their dark world well enough to move about. Discovering he could move from place to place, Dream Shadow searched for someone who could help he and his wife reach the surface of the world.

Eventually Dream Shadow and Shadow Woman found a friendly spirit who possessed great power and wisdom. This spirit was called Fire Maker. After they had become good friends, Dream Shadow asked Fire Maker if he could help them leave the world of darkness. Fire Maker said that anyone wishing to leave had to be able to see. Fire Maker and Dream Shadow paid a visit to Mud Snake. Dream Shadow traded his power of invisibility for the snake's power to see. Mud Snake happily traded his sight to Dream Shadow. That is why today earthworms have no eyes.

Seeing for the first time, Dream Shadow quickly realized they were living in the darkness of the world below. Dream Shadow asked Fire Maker to take him and his wife to the surface to live. Fire Maker told Dream Shadow they had to prove that they were worthy. The first test required Dream Shadow to bring light into the dark world below. From below, Dream Shadow studied the inhabitants of the surface. He enticed the Firefly to come down into the world of darkness to learn of secrets and stories. Firefly agreed and went down into the world of darkness.

Once there, he gathered his power and made a fire which awakened the first wind, which was called the North Wind. When Dream Shadow brought light to the dark world below it caused a hole to rip on the surface above. This opening not only allowed the night to escape from below, but it also released the North Wind to the upper world. Not realizing what he had done, Dream Shadow asked to take the second test.

The second test required Shadow Woman to create music in the land of darkness. She did this by bringing Snow Bird from the upper world and asked him to sing to her. The bird sang with such sad notes that it made the fire rocks cry. When the hot tears of the fire rocks touched the soil of the surface it caused an opening in the center of the earth. This opening released the South Wind into the world above.

The third test required Dream Shadow to defeat four evil spirits from the underworld. Dream Shadow and his wife fashioned a great jar, and then painted themselves inside it. That night when the four evil spirits arrived, they saw the pictures and rushed into the jar. Dream Shadow and his wife sealed the jar, and then asked Sun Bird to take it to the ends of the earth. When Sun Bird reached the ends of the earth, it released the four evils and they became the East Wind.

The final test was one of courage. The Giver of Life would allow Dream Shadow and his wife to leave the underworld if they could defeat the Water Witch. This they did with the help of their friend Fire Maker. When the Water Witch came to fight Dream Shadow, he ran across a huge hole which was covered. Once Dream Shadow was across, Water Witch followed. Halfway over the hole, the ground opened up and Fire Maker turned her into steam. This angry mist became the West Wind.

After its creation, the West Wind was so powerful it tore open a great gash in the earth's surface and destroyed the garden and all life that existed on it. When the Giver of Life took Dream Shadow and his wife to the surface, they found only a desert where the garden once stood. The Giver of Life asked the two if they wanted to go back to the safety of the underworld. They replied no.

Before he left, the Giver of Life warned Dream Shadow and Shadow Woman that the four winds had vowed vengeance on them. To help protect them, they were given twin sons. These two sons grew to build a house for their parents. They did this by using only basic elements. They took the earth (mud), rain (water) and straw (grass) and built the first house.

To further protect their parents, the sons gave the house strength of color. To insure stability, the sons centered the house with the powers of the earth. When Dream Shadow and Shadow Woman entered their home they knew they would always be safe from the revenge of the four winds.

In memory of Fire Maker, their protective friend from the world of darkness, they promised to always keep his presence (fire) in the center of their house. In this way they would honor his powerful spirit.

Native Americans used fire extensively. It was known as Our Grandfather Fire. The term implied respect. Fire was often used ceremonially. For important religious ceremonies sacred fires were kindled, and Indians used fires for hunting purposes. They used torches to blind deer and hunt fish close enough to spear from their canoes. Fire was also used as an instrument of war. Nomadic people burned off the grass and bush where they planned to put up lodges so that their enemies could not burn them out.